MISS HINDY'S CATS

Helena Clare Pittman

Carolrhoda Books, Inc./Minneapolis

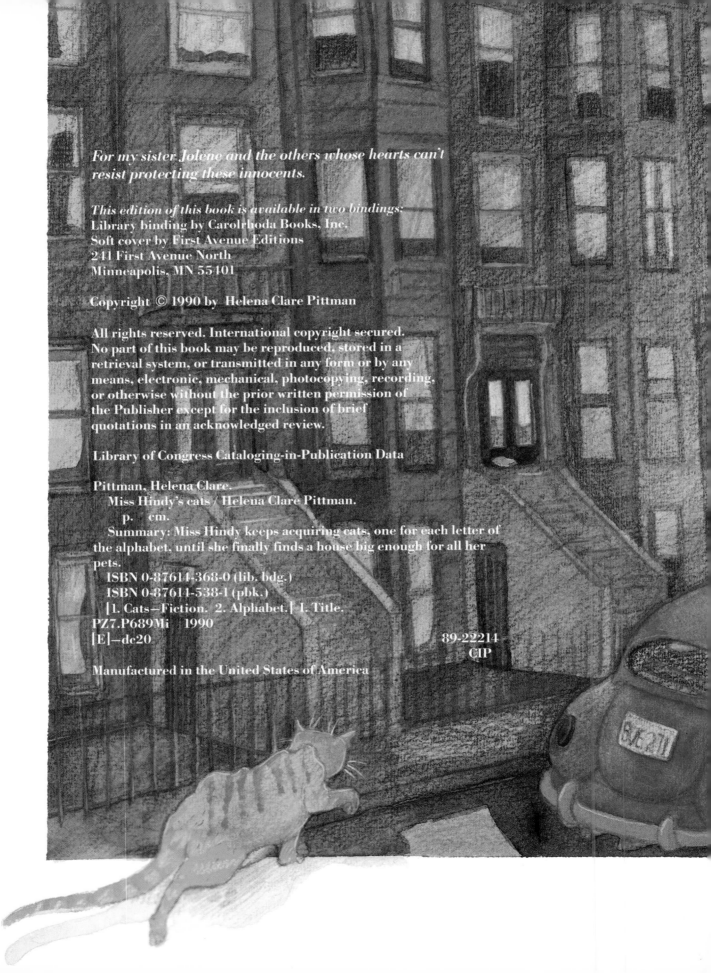

For my sister Jolene and the others whose hearts can't resist protecting these innocents.

This edition of this book is available in two bindings:
Library binding by Carolrhoda Books, Inc.
Soft cover by First Avenue Editions
241 First Avenue North
Minneapolis, MN 55401

Library of Congress Cataloging-in-Publication Data

Pittman, Helena Clare.
    Miss Hindy's cats / Helena Clare Pittman.
        p.   cm.
    Summary: Miss Hindy keeps acquiring cats, one for each letter of
the alphabet, until she finally finds a house big enough for all her
pets.
    ISBN 0-87614-368-0 (lib. bdg.)
    ISBN 0-87614-538-1 (pbk.)
    [1. Cats—Fiction. 2. Alphabet.] I. Title.
PZ7.P689Mi   1990
[E]—dc20
                                                    89-22214
                                                    CIP

Manufactured in the United States of America

This story first appeared in the July 1989 issue of *Cricket*, vol. 16, no. 11.

Miss Hindy had a cat. It showed up at her front door one morning, along with the newspaper.

Aa And it was still there when Miss Hindy put

on the porch light. Miss Hindy called her

Agnes for her favorite aunt.

Bb

She found Bella crouched under the rosebushes during a snowstorm. Her ears were delicate. Her nose was pink and velvety—too velvety to leave outside in the cold. So what could Miss Hindy do but take her in?

Cc

Chanticleer hobbled into the store where Miss Hindy shopped for vegetables. "Why, you have a splinter!" said Miss Hindy. She took him home and pulled it out. "Just a little soap and water and a dish of stew will put you right. You'll be as good as new in the morning."

Dd

Dagmar lay beside the road with a broken leg.

E e Edgar was chasing sparrows in the park.

F f Ferdinand had fallen into the lake.

Gg

Gretel got trapped on someone's roof.

Hh

Harold was a guest. A friend left him in Miss Hindy's charge during a cruise to the Virgin Islands, then found the climate irresistible.

Miss Hindy bought a new house.

Ii Jj

Isabelle and Jacqueline were
hard to tell apart. They arrived in the back of
the delivery truck that brought Miss Hindy's
coal. The delivery man had no idea where
they had come from.

K k

Kate found Miss Hindy at a train station. "That's no life for a cat!" said Miss Hindy.

Mm

Marybeth sat next to Miss Hindy at the circus.

Ll

Lilah showed up to tea.

Nn

Someone was chasing Nicholas Nickleby with a broom.

Oo

Oliver was tangled
in a fishing line.

What was Miss Hindy to do?

She moved again.

Pp

When Miss Hindy went to the theater,
Peter Piper was the last one out.
It was too late at night to leave him
crying on a busy street.

Qq

Quicksilver was napping at the zoo.

Rr

Mr. Roberts turned up on the Staten Island Ferry.

S s Snowflake followed Miss Hindy out of a department store.

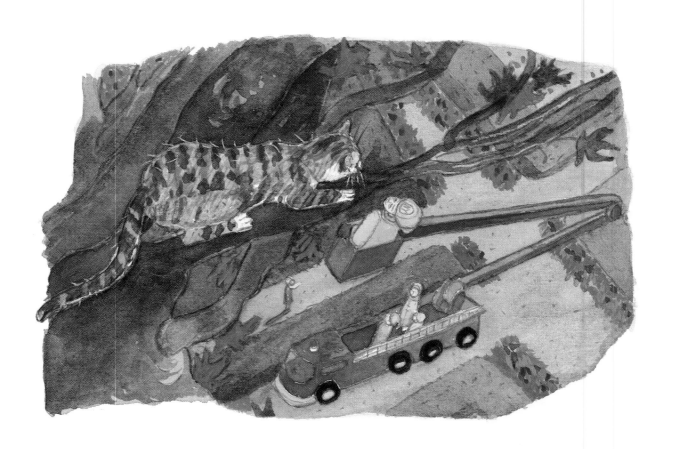

Tt
Tabitha was up a tree.

Uu

Ursula turned up in the ladies' room at the Tivoli Gardens.

Vv

Violet rode with Miss Hindy on the crosstown bus. She named him after her favorite flower.

Ww

Winifred made her home in the stacks of the public library. After all, she needed someplace to stay, until…

Xx Yy

Zz

Xavier, Yvonne, and Zinnia were old enough
to take care of themselves.

"We're all here!" said Miss Hindy, when all
at once there was a sound at the door.

"Oh my!" said Miss Hindy. "I'll have to give this some thought! But for now, come in—

Anton!"